WITHDRAWN

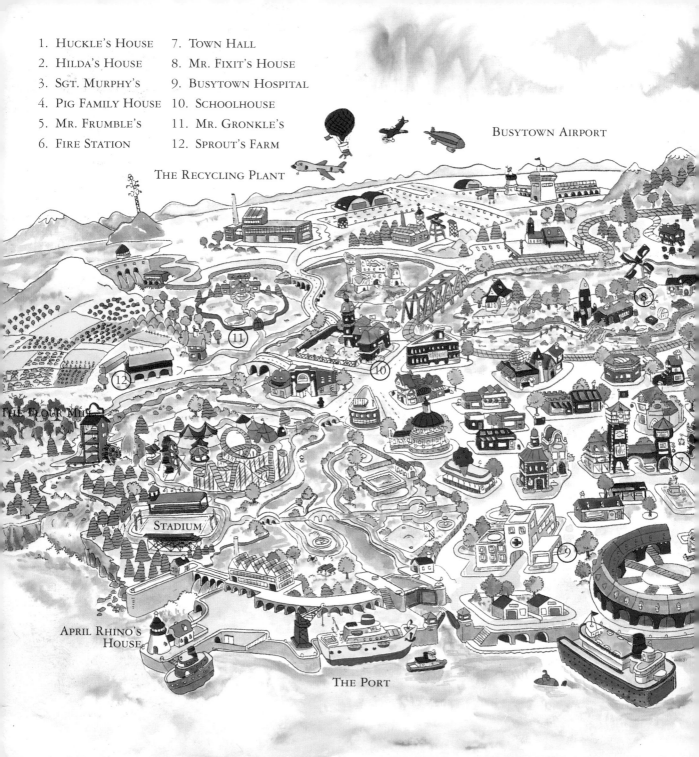

1. HUCKLE'S HOUSE
2. HILDA'S HOUSE
3. SGT. MURPHY'S
4. PIG FAMILY HOUSE
5. MR. FRUMBLE'S
6. FIRE STATION
7. TOWN HALL
8. MR. FIXIT'S HOUSE
9. BUSYTOWN HOSPITAL
10. SCHOOLHOUSE
11. MR. GRONKLE'S
12. SPROUT'S FARM

THE RECYCLING PLANT

BUSYTOWN AIRPORT

THE FLOUR MILL

STADIUM

APRIL RHINO'S HOUSE

THE PORT

First Aladdin Paperbacks edition August 1995
Copyright © 1994 by the Estate of Richard Scarry
Adapted from the animated television series
The Busy World of Richard Scarry™
produced by Paramount Pictures and Cinar.
Aladdin Paperbacks
An imprint of Simon & Schuster
Children's Publishing Division
1230 Avenue of the Americas
New York, NY 10020
Designed and produced by Les Livres du Dragon d'Or.
Printed in Italy.
10 9 8 7 6 5 4 3 2 1
ISBN 0-689-80369-9

The Busy World of Richard Scarry

Mr. Frumble's New Cars

Aladdin Paperbacks

Mr. Frumble drives his pickle car through Busytown. Suddenly, a gust of wind blows his hat off. "Oh dear!" says Mr. Frumble,

looking behind him. His hat is hooked on the tail of his car. He reaches out for it. "Ooops! Ahhh!"

Oh no! Look out, Mr. Frumble!
HONK! HONK!
Crassshhh!

"Don't worry, Mr. Frumble,"
Mr. Fixit assures him.
"I'll fix your car so that
it's better than new."

Sergeant Murphy
arrives at the
scene. "I'm sorry,
Mr. Frumble, but
I have to give
you a ticket.
It's the law."
"Oh dear,"
mutters Mr. Frumble.

UMFF!

Later that day, Mr. Frumble goes to Mr. Fixit's workshop.

"Your pickle car is ready, Mr. Frumble," Mr. Fixit says. "Well, thank you, Mr. Fixit."

Just then, Roger Rhino arrives in his bulldozer. His bulldozer needs a new scoop. "New scoop!" Mr. Fixit says. "I've got one in the back of my workshop." He turns to Mr. Frumble, "Why don't you take your pickle car for a test drive? You won't even recognize it!"

Mr. Frumble walks over to the pickle car. "But I recognize this car!" exclaims Mr. Frumble.

"It can't be mine—Mr. Fixit told me I wouldn't recognize it!" Then Mr. Frumble sees the bulldozer. He climbs on the seat, starts it up, and drives away.

"My goodness!" he says. "I certainly don't recognize this one."

Nearby, Sergeant
Murphy is helping
people cross the
busy street.

VROOM!
Watch out, Sergeant Murphy!

He jumps out of the way
just in time. That was a
close call!

"Help! Help, Sergeant Murphy!" shouts Roger Rhino.
"Mr. Frumble has taken my bulldozer!"
"He can't drive the bulldozer any better than he can drive his pickle car!" Sergeant Murphy says. "I'll have to give him another ticket!"

"Hmmm...I wonder what all these handles do..."
Mr. Frumble pulls and shoves. Clonk! Watch out! Mr. Frumble puts the
scoop down. **OOOOOPS! CRASH!** The scoop has dug up the street!

"Dear me!" Mr. Frumble exclaims. "Who put this big pile of dirt here?"

Soon a big crowd gathers on the square.
"What's happened?"
"Who dug this big hole?"
"Are they building a new town hall?"
people wonder.

What is everyone looking at? thinks
Mr. Frumble, walking toward a car
nearby.

He climbs
inside and
closes the
door.
Hilda hasn't
noticed that
her taxi has
a new driver!

HAILEY PUBLIC LIBRARY

Mayor Fox calls Sergeant Murphy from his office. "Get down here fast! Mr. Frumble just bulldozed the town square and has taken off in a taxi!"

"Oh no, now I have a taxi to catch!" Sergeant Murphy says, speeding away, his siren blaring.

Mr. Frumble looks at the taxi meter.

"What a noisy clock Mr. Fixit has installed. I better go back and get it fixed."

"But I need to go to the airport!" Hilda shouts.
"Hilda Hippo!" Mr. Frumble exclaims. "What a surprise."
"Mr. Frumble?" she says, puzzled. "I have to meet my cousin in ten minutes!"

"Well, in that case we had better step on it!" Mr. Frumble makes a U-turn and speeds away in the opposite direction.

CRASSHH! The car leaves the road.
Mr. Frumble drives through the fence to the airplane
and right up the loading ramp.

"AHHHHHHH!"
Hilda screams,
running away.

"I wonder where Hilda went," Mr. Frumble mutters.
Meanwhile, Rudolf von Flugel lands his airplane.
"Why is everyone in such a hurry?" Mr. Frumble wonders,
climbing into the driver's seat.

Up, up,
and away
he flies!

"Mr. von Flugel, have you seen
Mr. Frumble?" Sergeant Murphy
asks, arriving on his motorcycle.

"He just took off in my plane!"
Rudolf answers.

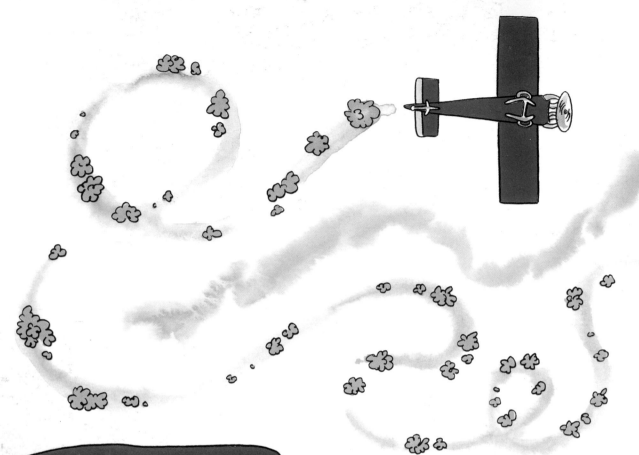

Rudolf's plane zooms through
the sky, zig-zagging, diving,
and looping-the-loop.
"My, what a smooth ride!"
Mr. Frumble exclaims.
Turning over, he loses his hat.
Oh no, not again, Mr. Frumble!
The plane dives through the sky.

"Now who would put a tree in the middle of the road?" wonders Mr. Frumble as the plane crashes through the branches.
THWASH!
Mr. Fixit runs up.
"Mr. Frumble! Are you all right?"
"Yes, Mr. Fixit," says Mr. Frumble, hanging from a branch. "Fine, thank you."

BUMP! THUMP! Down comes Mr. Frumble! And down comes his hat.

"Mr. Fixit," says Mr. Frumble, getting up, "do you remember you told me I wouldn't recognize my car? Well, I wonder if you could fix my car so I COULD recognize it?"

"I tried to tell you before," answers Mr. Fixit, pointing. "Your pickle car has been here all the time!"

SCREECH!
Sergeant Murphy pulls
up on his motorcycle.
"Now that I've caught up
with you, Mr. Frumble," he
says, "I have a few tickets
to give you!"
Sergeant Murphy pulls
out his ticket book:

"This one's for failure
to stop for an officer...
This one's for digging
a hole without a permit...
This one's for illegal
tree trimming..."

...and this one's for littering."
Poor Mr. Frumble!
"Dear me, I think I will go now," Mr. Frumble sighs.
He climbs into the driver's seat one more time.

"Wait! Mr. Frumble!" Sergeant Murphy shouts.

"That's MY motorcycle!"

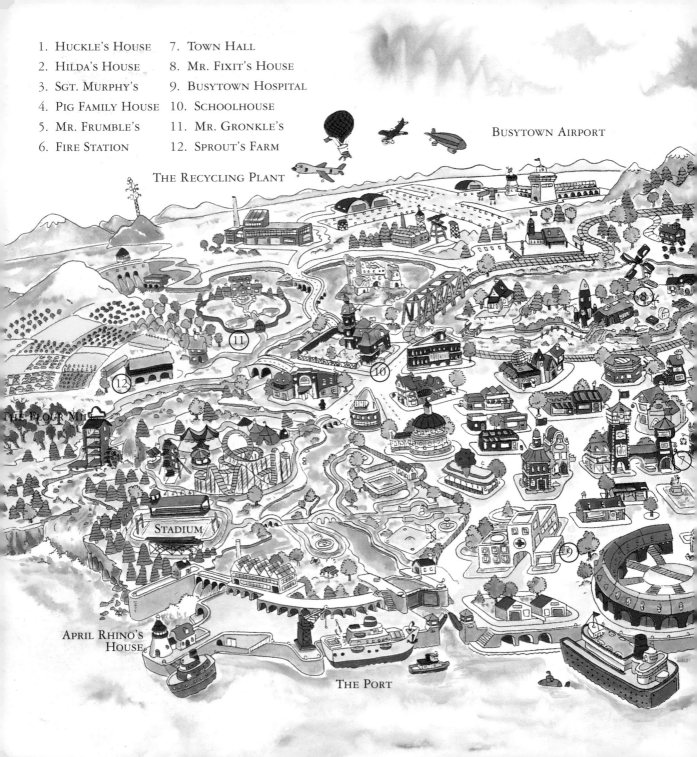

1. HUCKLE'S HOUSE
2. HILDA'S HOUSE
3. SGT. MURPHY'S
4. PIG FAMILY HOUSE
5. MR. FRUMBLE'S
6. FIRE STATION
7. TOWN HALL
8. MR. FIXIT'S HOUSE
9. BUSYTOWN HOSPITAL
10. SCHOOLHOUSE
11. MR. GRONKLE'S
12. SPROUT'S FARM

THE RECYCLING PLANT

BUSYTOWN AIRPORT

THE FLOUR MILL

STADIUM

APRIL RHINO'S HOUSE

THE PORT

Welcome to
Busytown!

MOUNT BUSY
OBSERVATORY

SKI CHALET

CAMPING GROUNDS

BUSY BAY
POINT

BRUNO'S
SNACK
STAND

THE BEACH

THE
TRAIN
STATION

BUSYTOWN GRAND HOTEL

SEA FORT